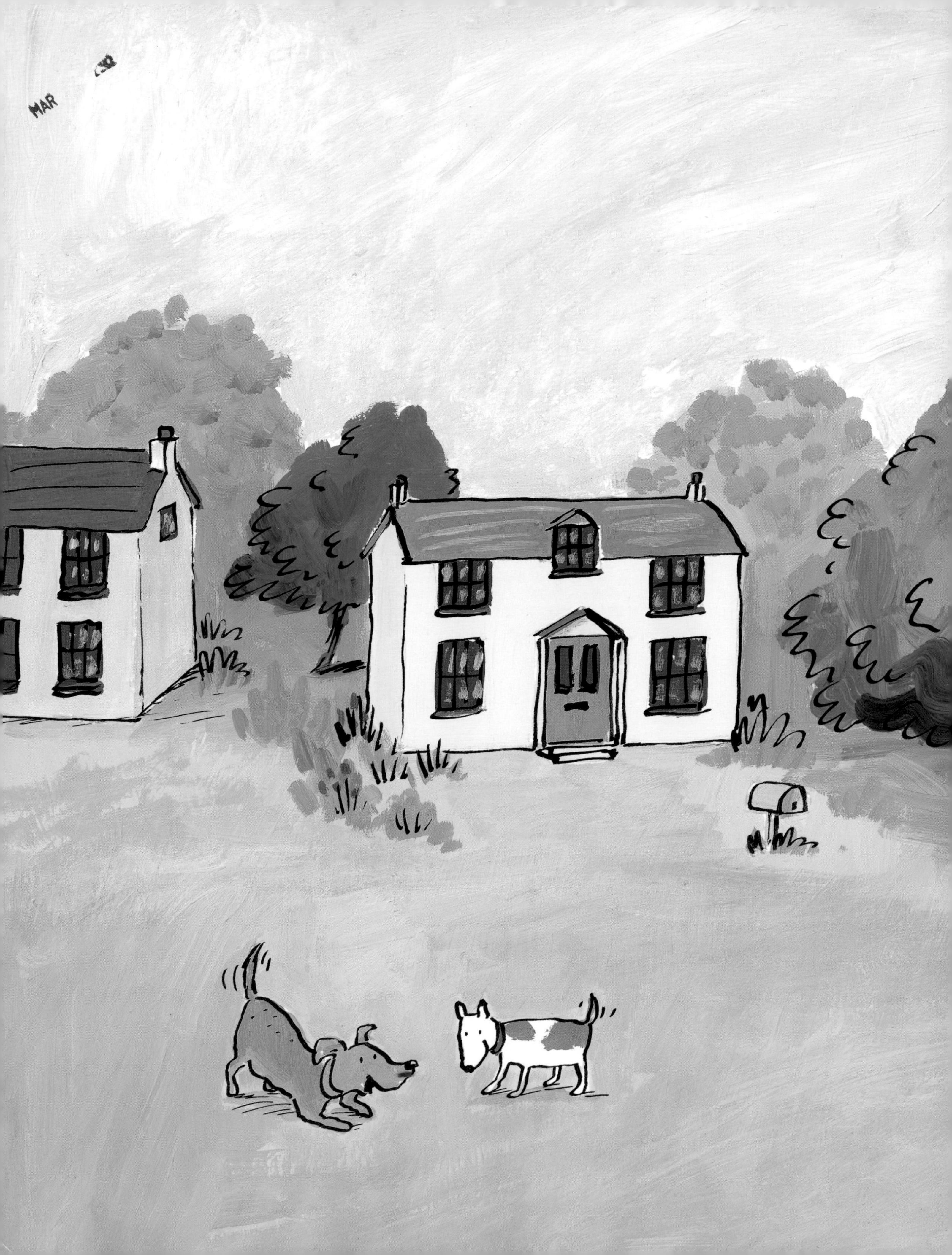
MAR

Murphy Meets the Treadmill

Harriet Ziefert

Illustrated by Emily Bolam

HOUGHTON MIFFLIN COMPANY BOSTON 2001

Walter Lorraine Books

For Esther Ehrlich
—H.Z.

Walter Lorraine ⟨wl⟩ Books

Text copyright © 2001 by Harriet Ziefert
Illustrations copyright © 2001 by Emily Bolam
All rights reserved. For information about permission
to reproduce selections from this book, write to:
Permissions, Houghton Mifflin Company
215 Park Avenue South, New York, New York 10003.

www.houghtonmifflinbooks.com

Library of Congress Cataloging-in-Publication Data

Ziefert, Harriet.
    Murphy meets the treadmill / written by Harriet Ziefert ; illustrated by Emily Bolam.
      p. cm.
    Summary: Having decided that her yellow Labrador is overweight, Cheryl puts him on
    a diet and makes him exercise, a program which has marvelous results.
    ISBN 0-618-11357-6
      [1. Labrador retreiver—Fiction. 2. Dogs—Fiction. 3. Weight control—Fiction. 4.
    Pets—Fiction.] I. Bolam, Emily, ill. II. Title.

PZ7.Z487 Muk 2001
[E]—dc21

                                                            00-044906
                                                            CIP

Printed in China for Harriet Ziefert, Inc.
HZI 10 9 8 7 6 5 4 3 2 1

Everyone calls me Murphy.
I live with Cheryl in an
old house with a large
front porch.

The porch is my favorite place to be.
I'm happy just to lie on the top step
and watch the people go by.

My favorite activity is eating.

I love food, especially between meals.
And lucky for me, there are lots of
people who like to feed me!

One day Cheryl told me I was getting fat. I was surprised. I thought I had a good build and was an excellent example of my breed. And I thought I was better looking than most of my yellow Labrador cousins.

Cheryl tried to put me on the scale, but I refused. I don't like scales—and what I weigh is my own business.

Cheryl and I got into a tug of war, and...

Cheryl fell down!

"Murphy!" she yelled. "You have thirty seconds to get on that scale."

"No more heaping portions!
It's low-fat chow for you."

"No more leisurely walks," said Cheryl.
"We're jogging!"

I knew she meant business. And I wasn't interested in being sent to the basement. So I got myself on the scale.

"Ninety-five pounds! You definitely need to diet!" Cheryl scolded.

"And no more after-dinner snacks!"

I begged for just a little something,
but Cheryl didn't offer me a single chip.

One day a delivery van arrived.
I barked. I growled.
I tried to look FEROCIOUS!

But the men unloaded
the machine anyway.

"This is for the two of us. It's a treadmill,"
said Cheryl. "We'll take turns. It will help
us both stay trim and fit."

There's no way I'm getting on that machine,
I thought. And I barked even louder
than I bark at the vacuum cleaner.

Cheryl didn't care what I thought.
She pushed me onto the treadmill.

I immediately got off.

Cheryl picked me up again.
"Now stay," she said firmly.
"STAY!"

I felt ridiculous. I didn't know whether to laugh or growl. So I began to walk.

"Keep walking," said Cheryl. "This is your warm-up. Concentrate. Stay to the center, so you don't fall off."

Cheryl turned up the machine,
and I had to walk a little faster.

I whimpered. I whined. But Cheryl
did not turn off the motor.

"There will be a nice drink of water
when you get off," said Cheryl.
"And then you can relax on the porch."

The thought of being able to
stretch out kept me going.

"Good dog," said Cheryl.
"You're almost done."

It wasn't long before word got out that I knew how to use a treadmill. Everyone wanted to see me doing my daily exercises, so Cheryl moved me to the porch.

The neighbors didn't stop talking.

When Nikka, the neighbor's hound, came
to check things out, I knew she thought
I was handsome. And physically fit.

And I said to myself,
Exercise is worth it!

The local newspaper sent a reporter and a photographer. I posed for pictures. Clearly, this was just the beginning. Soon I would be famous. AND RICH!

But I'll never forget my old friends!